#2 "Power Lines"
Stan Lee – Creator
Stuart Moore – Writer
P.H. Marcondes – Artist

PAPERCUTZ
New York

#2 "Power Lines"
Stan Lee – Creator
Stuart Moore – Writer
P.H. Marcondes – Artist
Andie Tong – Cover, Endpapers, and Character Profiles Artist
Jolyon Yates – Title Page Artist
Elaina Unger– Colorist
Bryan Senka – Letterer
Dawn Guzzo – Production
Melissa Kleynowski – Editorial Intern
Jeff Whitman – Editor
Jim Salicrup
Editor-in-Chief

ISBN: 978-162991-444-2 paperback edition
ISBN: 978-162991-445-9 hardcover edition

Papercutz books may be purchased for business or promotional use. For information on bulk purchases
please contact Macmillan Corporate and Premium Sales Department at (800) 221-7945 x5442.

Printed in Korea through Four Colour Print Group
November 2016 by WE SP Co., Ltd

Distributed by Macmillan
First Printing

PAPERCUTZ™

Disney Graphic Novels available from PAPERCUTZ

The power of the Zodiac comes from twelve pools of mystical energy. Due to a sabotaged experiment, twelve magical superpowers are unleashed on Steven Lee and twelve others.

TIGER

STEVEN

POWERS:

STRENGTH, REFLEXES

Now Steven Lee is thrown into the middle of an epic global chase. He'll have to master strange powers, outrun super-powered mercenaries, and unlock the secrets of the Zodiac Legacy. When Steven is first rescued by Jasmine and Carlos, he relishes his newfound powers and is excited to be on a grand adventure, alongside...

PIG

DUANE

POWERS:

INFORMATION PROCESSING

RAM

LIAM

POWERS:

INVULNERABILITY

RABBIT

KIM

POWERS:

TELEPORTATION

ROOSTER

ROXANNE

POWERS:

SONIC SCREAM

DRAGON

JASMINE

POWERS:
FIRE BREATHING, FLIGHT,
MIND CONTROL

The Vanguard organization is
bent on tracking down all of
the Zodiac powers. But one
of its own has joined Steven
Lee and friends...

OX

MALIK

POWERS:

STRENGTH

Steven and his
new friends will
need to stay one
step ahead of the
Vanguard...

The Vanguard are...

HORSE

JOSIE

POWERS:
**SUPER STRENGTH
AND ENDURANCE**

DRAGON

MAXWELL

POWERS:
**FIRE BREATHING, FLIGHT,
MIND CONTROL**

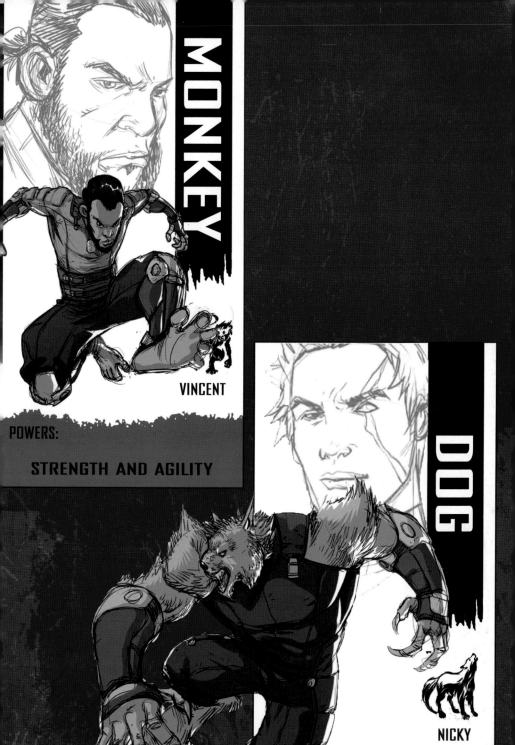

MONKEY

VINCENT

POWERS:

STRENGTH AND AGILITY

DOG

NICKY

POWERS:

ANIMAL TRANSFORMATION

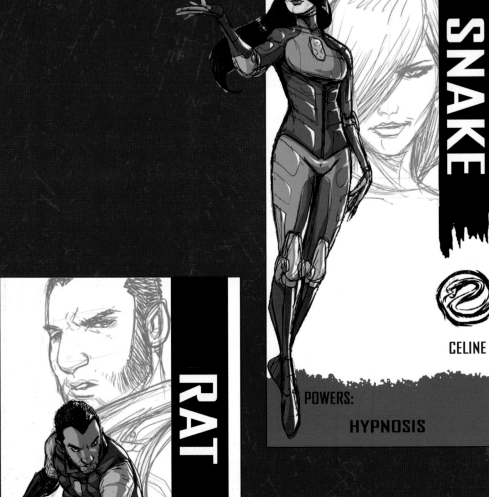

SNAKE

CELINE

POWERS:

HYPNOSIS

RAT

THIAGO

POWERS:

SUPERHUMAN REFLEXES,
INTUITION

WHOAAAAOAAAOOOOOOOAH!

MON DIEU! MON DIEU, ARRÊTEZ-LA! *

ELLE VA FAIRE DÉRAILLER LE TRAIN!**

*"MY GOD! MY GOD, STOP HER!"

**"SHE'S GOING TO DERAIL THE TRAIN!"

ROX --

I HEARD! I STOPPED! I STOPPED ALREADY!

PULL ME BACK IN!

UHHHH --

≋WHUFF!≋

THAT WAS CLOSE.

GOOD THING NOTHIN' CAN HURT ME.

OH, GREAT!

NOTHING CAN HURT YOU!

WHAT ABOUT ME?

OKAY. OPTIONS?

PREFERABLY *FAST* OPTIONS...

I HAVE ONE OTHER IDEA.

THIS IS A DARK-WEB INFOGRID SHOWING THE LEY LINES BENEATH THE EARTH'S SURFACE.

LEY LINES?

THAT'S JUST ANCIENT SUPER-STITION!

THE LEY LINES ARE REAL... AND THEY ARE LINKED WITH OUR OWN ZODIAC POWERS IN A WAY WE DON'T FULLY UNDERSTAND.

I MAY BE ABLE TO REACH OUT TO THEM WITH MY POWER, AND USE THEIR ENERGY TO SLOW THE TRAIN'S PROGRESS.

HOWEVER, IT WILL TAKE A FEW MINUTES.

NOUS N'AVONS PAS "A FEW MINUTES"! *

* "WE DON'T NOT HAVE (YOU KNOW THE RES

20

CAN WE HELP?

JUST LET ME WORK.

BIP BIP

WHAT IS IT, OX?

WE'RE A LITTLE BUSY HERE.

I CAN SEE THAT...

...I'M DIRECTLY ABOVE YOU.

THE PLANE'S ON AUTOPILOT, LOCKED TO THE TRAIN'S COURSE.

BUT YOU DON'T LOOK LIKE YOU'RE DOING TOO GOOD DOWN THERE.

SO I JUST WANTED TO ASK...

MALIK
The Ox
POWER: ENHANCED STRENGTH

...NEED ANY HELP?

YOU'RE HERE AS *BACKUP*, OX. *THAT'S ALL.*

IF WE NEED YOU--

WE'LL BE IN TOUCH.

Y'KNOW, WE PROBABLY *COULD* USE HIS HELP...

MAYBE.

BUT I'M NOT READY TO TRUST OX.

NOT YET.

22

THIRTY-SIX HOURS AGO THE ZODIACS' GREENLAND HEADQUARTERS...

OKAY. SO YOU'RE HERE.

WHY?

YOU WANT THE LONG OR SHORT ANSWER?

SHORT.

I WANT TO JOIN UP.

MATE?

I THINK WE'RE GONNA NEED THE LONG ANSWER.

STEVEN
The Tiger
POWERS: STRENGTH, ENHANCED REFLEXES

HERE'S THE THING, MAN: LAST YEAR YOU WERE WORKING FOR *MAXWELL*, OUR WORST ENEMY.

YOU REMEMBER MAXWELL? THE GUY WHO WANTS TO STEAL ALL OUR ZODIAC POWERS FOR HIMSELF?

KIM
The Rabbit
POWER: TELEPORTATION

SO WHY SHOULD WE TRUST YOU NOW?

HEY!

ARRHH!

SORRY.

OLD HABITS.

LISTEN. I'M HERE BECAUSE MAXWELL'S GONE TOO FAR.

I WAS TAUGHT: ANY MISSION WHERE YOU HAVE TO FIRE YOUR GUN IS A FAILURE.

MAXWELL DOESN'T AGREE -- HE'S A SHOOT-FIRST TYPE.

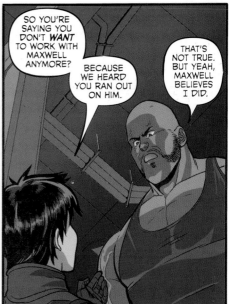

SO YOU'RE SAYING YOU DON'T *WANT* TO WORK WITH MAXWELL ANYMORE?

BECAUSE WE HEARD YOU RAN OUT ON HIM.

THAT'S NOT TRUE. BUT YEAH, MAXWELL BELIEVES I DID.

OKAY, FIRST OF ALL, THAT'S A PRETTY RIDICULOUS STORY.

COULDN'T YOU COME UP WITH SOMETHING BETTER?

LIKE, MAYBE YOU AND MAXWELL HAD A KICKBOXING FIGHT ON TOP OF A VOLCANO, WITH NINJA THROWING STARS?

AND LIGHT-SABERS.

ALWAYS THROW IN SOME LIGHT-SABERS.

SECOND: IT DOESN'T SOUND LIKE YOU'RE HERE BECAUSE YOU DON'T *WANT* TO WORK WITH MAXWELL ANYMORE.

IT SOUNDS LIKE HE KICKED YOUR BUTT TO THE CURB.

THAT'S NOT --

AND THIRD: YOU USED TO HIT ME.

A LOT.

25

I'M A SOLDIER.

I GET MY ORDERS, I CARRY 'EM OUT.

AND RIGHT NOW, MY ORDERS ARE TO STAY PUT.

THEY DON'T EVEN TRUST ME ENOUGH TO GIVE ME CONTROL OF THE PLANE.

AUTOPILOT LOCKED

I KNOW I COULD BE HELPING, DOWN THERE. BUT I HAVE MY ORDERS.

AND I'M A SOLDIER.

OR AM I SOMETHING ELSE, NOW?

VOUS NE POUVEZ TOUJOURS PAS COUPER LES MOTEURS? *

LE LOGICIEL EST SURCHARGÉ. CES CONTRÔLES SONT INUTILES! *

JE VOIS BIEN. **

* "THE SOFTWARE IS OVERLOADED. THESE CONTROLS ARE USELESS!"

* "YOU STILL CAN'T SHUT DOWN THE ENGINES?"

** "I CAN THA

THIS TRAIN IS HEADED FOR PARIS, AYE? IF WE PLOW INTO THE CITY AT THIS SPEED--

I WOULDN'T WORRY.

WE'RE GOING TO DERAIL AND CRASH LONG BEFORE THEN.

OH, THAT'S THE GOOD NEWS?

ANY LUCK WITH THE LEY LINES?

NO.

I CAN SEE THE ENERGIES, BUT I CAN'T HARNESS THEM.

THERE'S JUST TOO MUCH WE DON'T KNOW ABOUT THE ZODIAC POWER.

28

OKAY. WE CAN'T CUT THE ENGINES, AND WE CAN'T USE MYSTIC MUMBO-JUMBO ENERGY. IF WE TRY TO STOP THE TRAIN BY BRUTE FORCE, WE'LL TEAR IT APART.

WHAT DOES THAT LEAVE?

I'LL TELL YE WHAT IT LEAVES!

YOU TWO NEED TO GET OFF THIS TRAIN BEFORE IT CRASHES!

HAVE THE PLANE PICK YE UP. I'M INDESTRUCTIBLE-- I'LL STAY HERE AN' TRY TO--

AREN'T YOU FORGETTING SOMETHING, LIAM?

"THERE'S A HUNDRED AND THIRTY PEOPLE ON THIS TRAIN.

"AND THEY'RE COUNTING ON US!"

ONE HUNDRED THIRTY-ONE, ACTUALLY.

A WOMAN IN THE LAST CAR JUST HAD A BABY.

HOW CAN YE KNOW THAT?!

TWITTER--

THE POINT IS: WE CAN'T JUST LEAVE ALL THESE PEOPLE TO DIE.

29

ET
LE PANTO-
GRAPH? *

THE
PANTO-
GRAPH?

THE
PANTO-
GRAPH!

THE
WHIC
NOV

* "WHAT ABOUT THE PANTOGRAPH?"

I'LL
EXPLAIN
LATER.

WE'VE
GOT TO GET
UP TO THE
ROOF!

THE
ROOF?

THE, UH,
ROOF.

ALL
RIGHT.

NOW
YE'RE
TALKIN'!

HEY.

I COULDN'T SLEEP EITHER.

THANK YOU!

WOW. THAT BRINGS BACK MEMORIES.

YEAH. I USED TO REALLY SHRED IT ONSTAGE.

THEN I GOT MY ZODIAC POWER. AND IT WAS JUST TOO DANGEROUS FOR ME TO PLAY IN PUBLIC.

THAT SEEMS LIKE A LIFETIME AGO.

I KEEP THINKING ABOUT WHAT OX SAID, YOU KNOW?

THAT HE'S A DIFFERENT PERSON NOW, BUT HE DOESN'T KNOW WHO HE IS YET.

I FEEL THAT WAY TOO, SOMETIMES.

WHAT ABOUT OX? DO YOU TRUST HIM?

NOW WE'D LIKE TO DO A LITTLE NUMBER FOR ANYONE OUT THERE WHO FEELS A LITTLE DOWN...

I DUNNO.

I DON'T EITHER.

BUT PART OF OUR MISSION IS TO HELP PEOPLE WITH ZODIAC POWERS.

...ANYONE WHO FEELS LOST, WHO'S JUST BEEN THROUGH A BREAKUP, OR HAD A GOOD FRIEND MOVE AWAY.

SO I GUESS WE HAVE TO TRY.

ACTUALLY, I WANTED TO TELL YOU SOMETHING.

KIM'S LEAVING THE TEAM.

UN, DEUX, TROIS...

WHAT? FOR GOOD?

I DON'T KNOW. ER DAD'S PRETTY SICK

SO THE TEAM'S GONNA BE A LITTLE SHORT-HANDED FOR A WHILE.

♪ SEE THAT STARVING MAN ON THE TEN O'CLOCK NEWS ♪

BUT, HEY. WE CAN HANDLE IT.

WE'RE HEROES NOW, RIGHT?

♪ HE IS FEELING SO ALONE ♪

LOOK, WE'VE ALL GOT OUR OWN LIVES.

I HAVEN'T SEEN MY PARENTS FOR A YEAR. SOMETIMES I CAN BARELY REMEMBER WHAT THEY LOOK LIKE.

♪ THE WOMAN LIVING IN A SHELTER

THE MAN WHO HAS LOST HIS HOME ♪

I KNOW YOUR MOM WANTS YOU TO LEAVE THE TEAM.

AND YOU'VE PROBABLY LEARNED ENOUGH ABOUT YOUR POWERS TO USE THEM SAFELY NOW MAYBE EVEN ONSTAGE.

♪ YOU FEEL THE URGE TO HELP THEM

♪ BUT YOU DON'T KNOW HOW TO START ♪

BUT MAXWELL'S STILL OUT THERE. AND PEOPLE *NEED* HEROES -- WE'RE GETTING MORE CALLS FOR HELP, EVERY DAY.

SO PLEASE... THINK ABOUT IT BEFORE YOU BAIL, OKAY?

♪ JUST REEEEACH OUT ♪

GUESS IT ALL COMES BACK TO OX'S QUESTION.

WHO AM I, NOW?

♪ REACH OUT WITH YOUR HAND ♪

♪ REACH OUT AND TAKE A STAND ♪

THE ENGINEER SAYS HE CAN'T REDUCE THE PANTOGRAPH TENSION FROM INSIDE.

THE CONTROLS ARE COMPLETELY FUSED.

THEN IT'S UP TO US.

WAIT A MINUTE. HOLD ON.

WHAT ARE YOU DOING?

I'M GONNA *RAM* IT.

D-DID I MENTION THAT WIRE HAS OVER NINE HUNDRED VOLTS RUNNING THROUGH IT?

ARE YOU CLINICALLY INSANE?

40

YOU HAVE TO UNDERSTAND, I DIDN'T **ASK** FOR THE ZODIAC POWER.

IT ERUPTED OUT OF THESE MYSTIC POOLS IN CHINA, AND SOUGHT OUT PEOPLE TO HOST IT.

I DIDN'T EVEN WANT IT!

BUT NOW I'M PART OF A TEAM. AND PEOPLE ARE COUNTING ON US.

JUST THE OTHER DAY, WE SAVED A LOT OF PEOPLE FROM A SANDSTORM IN DUBAI.

NOW WE'RE SHORTHANDED. AND MORE RESCUE CALLS KEEP COMING IN.

SO I DON'T KNOW IF I EVEN HAVE THE RIGHT TO LEAVE.

IT'S JUST SO HARD.

I GUESS I NEED TO KNOW WHAT YOU THINK...

...MOM?

WELL, THIS IS A FIRST.

YOU'VE NEVER LISTENED TO ME BEFORE!

MAMAN--

I AM JUST TEASING YOU, DEAR.

I KNOW YOU'RE A SUPER PERSON NOW.

I KNOW YOU GO ON MISSIONS, THAT YOU JUMP OUT OF PLANES AND PARACHUTE INTO TSUNAMIS AND, I GUESS, PROBABLY FIGHT OTHER SUPER PERSONS TOO.

BUT IS THAT *REALLY* WHO YOU ARE?

EVER SINCE YOU WERE A TINY GIRL, MUSIC HAS BEEN THE MOST IMPORTANT THING IN YOUR LIFE.

SO IF YOU ARE REALLY, FOR THE FIRST TIME IN YOUR LIFE, ASKING WHAT *I THINK*...

I THINK IT SOUNDS AS IF YOU'RE TRYING TO CONVINCE YOURSELF OF SOMETHING.

47

ROX! WHAT, YE GOT YER PHONE OFF?

WE HAVE AN EMERGENCY.

A HIGH-SPEED TRAIN TRAVELING FROM STRASBOURG TO PARIS HAS GONE OUT OF CONTROL.

THE FRENCH GOVERNMENT HAS JUST CALLED FOR OUR ASSISTANCE.

EVERY SECOND COUNTS.

BUT-- WHERE'S STEVEN?

HE'S NOT AROUND.

LOOKS LIKE IT'S JUST US!

MAMAN?

OH, GO.

PEOPLE ARE COUNTING ON YOU, RIGHT?

THEN THAT JUST LEAVES OX.

AYE. HE'S A STRONG FELLA...

B-BUT WHERE IS HE? WHERE'S THE PLANE?

IT'S GONE!

I KNEW IT.

PEOPLE DON'T CHANGE

TH-THE PLANE WAS ON AUTOPILOT. WE DIDN'T EVEN PROGRAM IT TO OBEY OX'S COMMANDS...

I THINK WE'VE GOT A MORE URGENT PROBLEM RIGHT NOW.

LIKE, WE'VE PROBABLY GOT SECONDS LEFT TO LIVE!

WE'LL HAVE TO JUMP.

WITH OUR ZODIAC POWERS, WE MIGHT SURVIVE...

B-B- BUT WHAT ABOUT ALL THE PEOPLE ON THE TRAIN?

I DON'T KNOW--

JUST A BLOODY SECOND!

LIAM?

LOOK!

THE PLANE!

IT'S COMIN' OUT OF STEALTH MODE NOW--

--AND THERE'S OX!

HEADS UP--

WE'RE SLOWING DOWN...

HE DID IT.

OX DID IT.

YEAH -- *AFTER* HE VANISHED WITH THE PLANE, AND DIDN'T ANSWER OUR CALLS.

HE'S GOT SOME EXPLAINING TO DO.

LIAM, CAN YOU HEAR ME?

RENDEZ-VOUS WITH US AT THE TRAIN --

AH, THAT MIGHT BE A PROBLEM.

WHY? ARE YOU OKAY?

OF COURSE I'M OKAY--

IT'S JUST PRESSURE POINTS. I FIND HUMAN PHYSIOLOGY FAR EASIER TO UNDERSTAND...

...THAN HUMAN BEHAVIOR.

OKAY, OX.

TIME FOR SOME ANSWERS.

FIRST OFF: HOW DID YOU MOVE THE PLANE?

I KNOW WHERE THE OVERRIDES ARE.

THIS PLANE USED TO BELONG TO MAXWELL, REMEMBER? I'VE FLOWN IT DOZENS OF TIMES.

AND ARE YOU STILL?

WORKING FOR MAXWELL?

FOR THE HUNDREDTH TIME:

NO.

OKAY, SO YOU OVERRODE THE AUTOPILOT. WHY?

WHY?

SO I COULD *HELP* YOU!

LIAM. TELL HER --

YOU HAD THE STEALTH SHIELD ON, MATE. THERE WAS NO REASON T'DO THAT. THE LOCALS HAD SEEN THE PLANE ALREADY.

JUST AN OLD HABIT.

IT WAS STANDARD PROCEDURE, BACK WHEN I WORKED FOR... UH...

FOR MAXWELL.

MAYBE HE WAS TRYING TO STEAL THE PLANE.

IF I'D WANTED TO STEAL THE PLANE, IT'D BE GONE. AND SO WOULD I.

AYE, THAT MAKES SENSE.

LOOK. YOU WANT TO KNOW THE TRUTH?

I *THOUGHT* ABOUT STEALING THE PLANE.

I ALSO THOUGHT ABOUT DOING EXACTLY WHAT I WAS TOLD. STAYING UP THERE, FLYING IN CIRCLES, ACCOMPLISHING NOTHING.

I USED TO BE A SOLDIER. WHEN I WORKED FOR MAXWELL, I OBEYED ORDERS, NO MATTER WHAT.

BUT TODAY, I *DISOBEYED* ORDERS. BECAUSE I KNEW IT WAS THE RIGHT THING TO DO.

I DON'T KNOW WHAT THAT MAKES ME, NOW.

BUT I GUESS IT'S WHO I AM.

I KNOW.

IT MAKES YOU A HERO.

BEEP

BEEP

BEEP

...NOTHER ALL FOR HELP...

FROM REYKJAVIK, ICELAND. THERE'S A MASSIVE FLOOD IN THE MIDDLE OF THE CITY.

ICELAND'S A DETOUR, BUT IT'S ALONG OUR COURSE. I CAN HAVE US THERE IN LESS THAN AN HOUR.

WHAT DO YE SAY, BOSS?

The saga continues in *The Zodiac Legacy Volume 2: The Dragon's Return* on sale now!

WATCH OUT FOR PAPERCUTZ™

me to the super-speedy second THE ZODIAC ·Y graphic novel series, created by Stan Lee, n by Stuart Moore, and illustrated by P.H. ondes, from Papercutz—those subway-riding, commuters dedicated to publishing great ic novels for all ages. I'm Jim Salicrup, ·-in-Chief and brother of Bill Salicrup, a me MTA (Metropolitan Transit Authority) worker. t to talk a little bit about trains, but if I may I my train of thought a little, there's something should mention first...

ODIAC LEGACY began as a series of novels shed by Disney, written by Stan Lee and Stuart e, and profusely illustrated by Andie Tong. And I mean graphic novels, although there are plenty eat illustrations in each book by the awesome Tong. I mean prose novels, in which the story d primarily through words written by smiling Lee and studious Stuart Moore. Now, Papercutz s us!) has been working with the wonderful at Disney for years, publishing DISNEY FAIRIES ring Tinker Bell, and when we decided to add onal Disney titles to our ever-expanding rcutz line-up of graphic novels, we couldn't asking if we could create a graphic novel s based on the best-selling THE ZODIAC LEGACY.

Well, obviously the answer was yes, and we really lucked out in getting the self-same Stuart Moore to agree to write the graphic novels! What sly Stuart has cleverly done is to have the Papercutz graphic novels fit seamlessly into the continuity of the prose novels. So, THE ZODIAC LEGACY graphic novel #1 "Tiger Island" fits between the first and second prose novel, and the graphic novel, "Power Line," fits snuggly between two chapters in the second prose novel (we'll let you have fun figuring out exactly which two chapters). And for those of you who may not have picked up the prose novels yet, here's what you've been missing...

On sale from Disney Press:
The bestselling THE ZODIAC LEGACY novels!

Written by **Stan Lee & Stuart Moore**
Art by **Andie Tong**

COMING SOON

Volume 1
CONVERGENCE
Steven Lee discovers the power of the Zodiac, and becomes part of a fantastic new team!

Volume 2
THE DRAGON'S RETURN
With Steven's team falling apart, the evil Maxwell launches his ultimate plan to steal the Zodiac powers!

Volume 3
BALANCE OF POWER
Stripped of their powers, Steven and the Zodiacs must prevent the Dragon from destroying the world!

> AT LEAST THEY SPELLED MY NAME CORRECTLY!

st look at Stan Lee's face and you can tell he's nking, "Those guys and gals at Papercutz sure now what they're doing—this graphic novel is REAT!" Or at least that's what it looks like to us.

Gee, there's not much room left to talk about trains, is there? Well, I just have to squeeze this in: When artist P. H. Marcondes first started working for Papercutz, he drew THE HARDY BOYS graphic novels for years, and the very first HARDY BOYS graphic novel he contributed to featured a mystery that involved a runaway train! The story was called "The Opposite Numbers...," wherein Frank and Joe Hardy meet the deadly Noir Sisters. And that story, as luck and fate would have it, is included in THE HARDY BOYS ADVENTURES #1, a collected edition featuring four fantastic cases starring the teen sleuths, that's on sale now! (Guess that story was good *train*ing for THE ZODIAC LEGACY, eh?)

We hope you enjoyed "Power Lines" and you'll be back for THE ZODIAC LEGACY #3 "The Age of Bronze"!

Thanks,

Jim

STAY IN TOUCH!

EMAIL: salicrup@papercutz.com
WEB: papercutz.com
TWITTER: @papercutzgn
FACEBOOK: PAPERCUTZGRAPHICNOVELS
FANMAIL: Papercutz, 160 Broadway, Suite 700, East Wing, New York, NY 10038

STAN LEE
Creator

As if co-creating the Marvel Universe with suc characters as Spider-Man, The Avengers, The X-I Daredevil, The Incredible Hulk, Dr. Strange, an countless others, wasn't enough, Stan created a generation of heroes with THE ZODIAC LEGACY

STUART MOORE
Writer
Co-Author of THE ZODIAC LEGACY prose novels, Stuart is a writer and an award-winning comics editor.

P.H. MARCONDES
Artist
P.H. has been with Papercutz almost since the beginning illustrating such best-selling titles as THE HARDY BOYS, LEGO® NINJAGO, and SABAN'S THE POWER RANGERS.

ANDIE TONG
Cover Artist
Illustrator of THE ZODIAC LEGAC prose novel, he's a comic artist, multi-media designer, and book illustrator.

Donald L. Gelpi

COMMITTED
WORSHIP

A Sacramental Theology
for Converting Christians

Volume I
Adult Conversion and Initiation